Nathaniel Fludd

Nathaniel Fludd
BEASTOLOGIST

BOOK TWO

THE
BASILISK'S
LAIR

BY R. L. LaFEVERS

ILLUSTRATED BY KELLY MURPHY

sandpiper

HOUGHTON MIFFLIN HARCOURT
BOSTON   NEW YORK

All rights reserved. Published in the United States by Sandpiper, an
imprint of Houghton Mifflin Harcourt Publishing Company. Originally
published in hardcover in the United States by Houghton Mifflin
Books for Children, an imprint of Houghton Mifflin Harcourt
Publishing Company, 2010.

SANDPIPER and the SANDPIPER logo are trademarks of Houghton
Mifflin Harcourt Publishing Company.

For information about permission to reproduce selections from this
book, write to Permissions, Houghton Mifflin Harcourt Publishing
Company, 215 Park Avenue South, New York, New York 10003.

www.hmhbooks.com

The text of this book is set in ITC Giovanni.
The illustrations are pen and ink.

The Library of Congress has cataloged the hardcover edition as follows:
La Fevers, R. L. (Robin L.)
The basilisk's lair / by R. L. LaFevers ; illusrations by Kelly Murphy.
p. cm. — (Nathaniel Fludd beastologist ; bk. 2)

Summary: The continuing adventures of beastologist-in-
training, Nathaniel Fludd, as he accompanies his intrepid
Aunt Phil on a dangerous mission across West Africa to find
a deadly basilisk that is missing and begins to find clues
relating to the mysterious disappearance of his parents.

[1. Adventure and adventurers—Fiction. 2. Aunts—Fiction. 3. Basilisks
(mythical animals)—Fiction. 4. Animals, Mythical—Fiction. 5.
Orphans—Fictions. 6. Africa, West—Fiction.] I. Murphy, Kelly, 1977–
ill. II. Title.   PZ7.L1414Bas 2010
[Fic]—dc22   2009049705

ISBN: 978-0-547-23867-8 hardcover
ISBN: 978-0-547-54957-6 paperback

Manufactured in the United States of America
DOC 10 9 8 7 6 5 4 3 2 1
4500280559

THE
BASILISK'S
LAIR

Chapter One

Perched atop his camel, Nathaniel Fludd plodded through the desert sand. He did his best to ignore the merciless sun beating down on him.

Beastologist, he thought, trying out the title. *I am a beastologist.* One week ago, he'd been a castoff, unwanted by just about everybody. Now he was a beastologist-in-training. He imagined introducing himself. *"Why yes, Nathaniel Fludd here. Pleased to meet you. What's that? Oh, I'm a beast-ologist."* The faces around him would look duly impressed.

Aunt Phil's dry voice poked through his daydream. "This might be a good time to check your headings."

"What?"

"The headings?" she reminded him. "You're supposed to be navigating the way back to Wadi Rumba."

Nate looked down at the compass in his hand. The needle pointed to the north, but there was no town where it should be. He shook the compass, hoping maybe that would help.

"It's not stuck, Nate," Aunt Phil said. "Think. What did I tell you about north?"

"That the compass needle always points there?" He tried to keep the frustration out of his voice.

"And what else?"

Nate sighed. He was tired and his brain felt as fried as a breakfast egg from the heat of the Arabian sun. He wasn't interested in learning how to navigate right now. All he wanted was someplace cool to lie down. And water—an entire tub full of ice cold water.

But Aunt Phil was relentless. Once she had gotten it in her head that Nate was to learn how to use the compass, that had been it. He was in charge of getting them back to

Wadi Rumba. The problem was, he was failing miserably. He scrunched up his brain, trying to remember everything she'd told him. "Oh!" He remembered something. "Are we still above the equator? Because maybe I got that backwards."

Before Aunt Phil could answer, Greasle poked her head out of his rucksack. "Why're we stopped here?"

Aunt Phil glanced at the tiny gremlin. "Just orienting ourselves," she said.

"Well, hurry up already," Greasle said, but softly, so Aunt Phil wouldn't hear.

Nate glanced back at the compass. The needle had moved a few degrees to the east. He frowned at Greasle. "Get back in the pack. You're making the needle jump again."

"Sorry," she muttered. "I likes it better in the pack anyway."

Nate immediately felt guilty for snapping at her. She was his best friend, after all. His only friend, really. And it wasn't her fault they were off course. At least, he didn't think it was her fault. "Could Greasle's effect on the compass have put us off course?" he asked.

Aunt Phil shook her head. She didn't look hot or tired

at all. "No—as long as the gremlin stays in the pack where she belongs, she has no effect on the compass. We're off course because you didn't allow for the difference between true north and magnetic north."

"Oh yeah." He'd completely forgotten about that part. Nate looked around. Nothing but miles of sand and scorching heat. His first test at a true Fludd skill and he'd failed.

But maybe now Aunt Phil would take over. He looked at her hopefully.

She shook her head. "No, Nate. We learn best from our mistakes. I'm willing to bet you'll never forget the magnetic north differential again. However, in the interest of time, I will tell you that you need to adjust by four degrees to the east."

Nate grit his teeth, then set the outside ring on the compass four degrees to the east. As he looked up to reorient himself, he saw a cloud of dust coming toward them. "Look," he said.

Aunt Phil lifted the binoculars from around her neck. "Riders," she said after a moment. "Looking for us, it seems."

"How can you tell that?" he asked. Her skills never ceased to amaze him.

She lowered the binoculars and smiled. "Because they're waving. Come on. Let's ride out to meet them. They weren't scheduled to come looking for us for another two days."

"Then why are they here?"

"That's what I want to find out," she said. "Something must have come up."

Nate's heart sank at the cheerful *oh good, an exciting new disaster* tone in his aunt's voice. It could mean only one thing: trouble.

Chapter Two

*W*HEN THE MEN REACHED THEM, Nate saw one was waving a piece of paper in his hand.

"Omar, what brings you out here?" Aunt Phil asked.

Omar answered in breathless Arabic, then thrust the paper at Aunt Phil. "A telegram?" She frowned, then began to read aloud:

"For Phil Fludd. STOP. Urgent. STOP. Need help. STOP. Basilisk has escaped. STOP. Come to Bamako at once. STOP. Will await your arrival. STOP."

By the time she was done, Aunt Phil's tan face had paled. Since she was normally fearless, Nate knew this was a bad sign. "What's a basilisk?" he asked in a small voice.

"The king of serpents," she said shortly. She grew quiet after that, staring at the telegram for a few more moments, thinking. "Well, you're in luck," she finally said. "Your compass lesson is over. We've no time to waste. We must get back to Wadi Rumba at once." With that, she urged her camel into a gallop.

Nate sighed and looked down at his own camel. "I think that means we're supposed to run, too," he explained to Shabiib.

Shabiib gave him a sly smile.

"*Hut hut hut*," Nate said halfheartedly.

Shabiib did nothing.

Nate looked up to where Aunt Phil and the messengers had disappeared in a cloud of dust. "*Hut hut hut*," he repeated, this time applying his heels to the camel's flanks. The camel began walking, but it was nowhere near a gallop. At this pace they'd catch up to Aunt Phil sometime next week.

Nate's rucksack rustled behind him, and then the camel

gave a surprised snort and bolted forward. It was all Nate could do to hang on and keep his seat. When he was sure he wouldn't fall off, he risked a look behind him.

Greasle's little batlike face was smiling as she held up her two pincer fingers. "I didn't want to get left out here because of a stupid camel," she said. "I want back on me plane."

Shabiib never did catch up with the others, but Nate was able to follow their thick dust cloud. They reached Wadi Rumba in less than an hour, so they hadn't been too far off course. Heartened by this, Nate steered Shabiib to the camel pen. After he dismounted, he grabbed his rucksack and went to find Aunt Phil.

She had already set up one of the tents as a command post. He found her there, barking out orders. "Tell them it needs to be in Cairo by the day after tomorrow. No later!"

Before Nate could even ask what *it* was, another man rushed into the tent. "You wish to send a telegram?"

"Yes. To the British Mail Service in Cairo. 'Will arrive late tomorrow afternoon. STOP. Will need 450 gallons of fuel. STOP. Will take off day after that. STOP.' That's all," she said. The man nodded and scurried away.

"Ah, Nate. There you are." Aunt Phil motioned him over to the table where she had a large map laid out. "The basilisk lives in a remote area of the Sudan. Unfortunately, there are no planes or refueling facilities in West Africa. Our only chance to load up on fuel will be here." She placed her finger on a tiny dot. "The British airmail facility just outside Cairo should be able to supply us with all we need. We can make it from Cairo to Bamako in one run without refueling, but just barely. And we'll have to carry enough fuel in the cargo hold for our return trip." She glanced outside the tent opening. "I'm tempted to leave tonight, except they won't have our supplies ready. Besides, flying at night is a bit dicey. Why don't you get some sleep while I finish seeing to the arrangements?"

"Can you tell me about the basilisk?" Nate asked.

"I've too much to do just now," she said, not meeting his eye. She busied herself rolling up the map, stuffed it into a pack, and left the tent without another word.

As Nate plopped down onto one of the cushions, Greasle crawled out of his rucksack. "Is she gone?" the little gremlin asked, stretching her monkeylike body.

"You should stop worrying," Nate said. "I don't think she dislikes you quite so much anymore. She's beginning to see how useful you can be." Aunt Phil thought gremlins were pests, like rats or cockroaches. She hadn't been happy when Nate had first adopted Greasle as his pet.

Greasle snorted but looked pleased as well. "Wonder why she won't tell you about the basilick. Think she's hiding something?" she asked.

"A basilisk," Nate corrected, shifting uneasily on his cushion. "I don't *think* she's hiding anything." But the truth was, he had been wondering the exact same thing.

"Well, we doesn't have to waits for her, do we? Let's have a look."

Before Nate could protest, Greasle scampered over to one of Aunt Phil's saddlebags. Her nimble fingers closed around *The Book of Beasts*. It was bigger than she was, and she strained and tugged, trying to pull it out. "I could use some help here," she said.

"I'm not sure we should be doing this," Nate said.

"Course we should. You're a beastologist, ain't you? You don't needs no permission to look at a dumb old book. Or are you afraid?" Greasle had managed to work the book free by this time. It teetered on the edge of the pack, then tipped over, squashing her flat under its heavy weight. "Help!" she squeaked.

Nate quickly snatched up the book.

"Took you long enough," she sniffed, brushing herself off. "Now, let's look up the basil lick."

"*Basilisk*," Nate corrected, his fingers itching to open the book.

"Go on," Greasle urged.

Nate settled himself back down on the cushion and opened the book to *B. Basilisk*, the first entry.

Born from a cockerel egg and hatched by a serpent during the days of Sirius (the dog star), the basilisk is the most venomous creature on earth. Its gaze can strike a man or beast dead at twenty paces. Its breath is so poisonous that it causes trees and shrubs to wither and die on contact. It can make birds fall lifeless from the sky merely by spitting its venom into the air.

Greasle squealed in dismay and huddled closer to Nate.

This snakelike creature is not more than twenty fingers long, but do not be fooled by its small size. It has the head and legs of a rooster, and wings, too—only not of feathers, but of reptilian skin. His tongue is forked, and the tail ends in an arrow point. Like many poisoned things, he is brilliantly colored; his scales glitter like rubies, emeralds, and sapphires in the sunlight.

20 Fingers

B

BASILISK

Basilisk's venom is considered highly valuable by those who practice the dark arts as it is an undetectable poison.

The creature's scales and fangs also have great value

Nate studied the picture on the facing page. It was ugly, yet strangely beautiful, too. The beast had wicked-looking spines along its back, and its thick tail coiled round and round, like a snake, ending in a bright red point. It was covered in scales, not feathers, and had a cock's comb atop its head and a sharp yellow beak. Below the drawing, a separate note was handwritten in the margin.

"Basilisk's venom is considered highly valuable by those who practice the dark arts, as it is an undetectable poison. The creature's scales and fangs also have great value."

Nate stopped reading and closed the book. His hands trembled as he stuffed it back into Aunt Phil's saddlebag. No wonder she hadn't wanted to tell him about the basilisk! All his excitement at being a beastologist fled, leaving a cold lump of fear in its place.

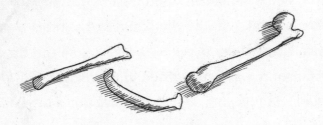

Chapter Three

*N*ATE SLEPT HORRIBLY. He'd dreamed he was being chased by a serpentlike bird that kept spitting poison at him. He was actually glad when Aunt Phil woke him and bundled him into the plane. They took off just as the first rays of the sun broke over the horizon.

The coolness of the morning quickly wore off and the plane became unbearably hot. Nate envied Greasle, who spent the whole trip curled up in his rucksack, fast asleep.

The landing in Cairo was the first time Nate had ever landed on a real airstrip, so it was much smoother than their other landings. He was surprised, however, by the facilities. Even though it was near a big city, the mail service was nothing but a cluster of dusty tents and a large metal shack. One other plane sat off to the side. As he and Aunt Phil climbed out of their cockpit, a young man dressed in khakis hurried forward.

"Dr. Fludd? I'm James Pickle. The British Mail Service has assigned me to assist you during your layover here in Cairo."

"What kind of name is Pickle, I'd like to know?" Greasle whispered in Nate's ear. He thought that was funny coming from someone named after grease.

"You mean you're here to see I don't upset the mail-service routine," Aunt Phil corrected.

"Not at all, Dr. Fludd." Mr. Pickle practically bowed in his eagerness to please. "Just to see that all your arrangements go smoothly and you find everything you need. In fact, we've gathered all the fuel you've requested. It's over here in the small hangar, if you'd like to come see for yourself."

"Very well. Lead the way."

As Mr. Pickle began marching toward the hangar, Aunt Phil lagged behind, letting Nate catch up to her. "You keep

that gremlin out of sight, Nate. The British Mail Service will never forgive me if I bring a gremlin into their midst and allow it to start mucking up their planes."

"How do they even know about gremlins?" Nate asked.

"Because airplane pilots were the ones who discovered them. And I'm whom they call to get *rid* of these pests." She gave Greasle a pointed glare, then hurried to catch up to Mr. Pickle.

They spent the rest of the afternoon inspecting fuel cans, supervising their loading into the fuselage, and pouring over an aeronautical map. It was the oddest map Nate had ever seen. Long and narrow, it was mounted on a pair of scrolls set in a wooden box with a compass at the top. "I'll keep this in my lap as we fly," Aunt Phil explained. "But I'll need your help as well. See those lines?"

Nate stared at the series of thin green lines she was pointing to. "Yes."

"Those are navigating furrows that have been plowed in the sand. It can be tricky to fly over featureless desert, so those furrows will help us navigate. We'll need to keep them in our sights at all times as we cross the Sahara. That will be your job."

When the sun finally set, Aunt Phil sent Nate to the small tent that had been assigned to them. It was hot and stuffy inside. Someone had left a plate of sandwiches for their dinner. Even though they were covered with wax paper, the sandwiches were dried out and stale. But they were better than nothing, Nate thought. And at least they were something he recognized.

After eating one of the sandwiches, he broke the second one into pieces for Greasle, who picked at it. With nothing else left to do, he crawled onto one of the cots. He was tired of sleeping on the ground and on strange, lumpy cots. Even the unfamiliar bed back at Aunt Phil's house would have been better than this. But what he really and truly wished for was his very own bed in his very own house. He wondered if he would ever see it again.

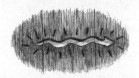

Nate awoke to the sound of Aunt Phil packing up her things. He blinked twice, then rubbed his eyes and sat up, nearly tumbling Greasle to the floor.

"Watch it!" she cried, clinging to the blanket for dear life.

"Sorry." He scooped her back up and set her carefully on the cot. "Morning," he said to Aunt Phil.

"Morning, Nate. I repacked your things while you were sleeping. Added a few supplies I thought you'd need."

"Thanks." He jumped off the cot and stuffed his feet into his shoes. During the night, he had come up with a plan. Since this basilisk was such a dangerous beast, Nate knew he would only get in Aunt Phil's way. Clearly it would be best if he caught a mail plane back to England and waited for her there. Nate couldn't wait to suggest his plan, but before he could say anything, there was a tapping at the tent door.

It was Mr. Pickle, inviting them to the mess tent for one last hot breakfast.

"I'm afraid I've too much to do," Aunt Phil told him. "But if you would take Nate, I'm sure he would appreciate a hot meal."

Nate could tell that Mr. Pickle wanted to argue, but his desire to please won out in the end. "Very well, Dr. Fludd. Nathaniel? This way, if you please."

Nate grabbed his rucksack and followed Mr. Pickle to a

wide canvas tent. Like everything else, it was covered with a thick layer of reddish sand. Inside, a large burly man was slinging runny-looking eggs onto tin plates. Nate took one and followed Mr. Pickle to an empty table.

Nate's stomach was so full of excitement for his new plan that there wasn't any room for breakfast. He picked at his eggs and tried to work up his courage. When Mr. Pickle was almost finished with his breakfast, Nate finally asked, "Do you know where I can make arrangements for a flight back to England?"

Mr. Pickle looked a bit confused. "Aren't you going with Dr. Fludd?"

"I . . . we . . . thought it best if I returned to England for now. That way she can focus all her attention on her mission."

Mr. Pickle thought for a moment, and Nate held his breath. "I suppose that makes sense. There's no ticket office or anything like that. Your best bet would be to check with the pilots awaiting their takeoffs. One of them might have some extra room."

Nate let out a whoosh of relief. "Thank you, sir." Nate pushed his plate away and stood up to leave.

Once outside, he looked around, trying to get his bearings. Greasle poked her head out of his rucksack. "Won't that aunt of yours be peeved?" she asked.

"She *shouldn't* be," Nate said. "I'm making all the arrangements myself and saving her any trouble." Besides, he was sure she'd agree once he had had a chance to explain it to her. And if he could present it as something already arranged, so much the better.

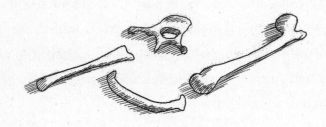

Chapter Four

*T*HERE WERE TWO OTHER PLANES besides Aunt Phil's waiting near the hangar. One of them had just landed and a pilot was disembarking. Squaring his shoulders, Nate approached him. "Excuse me?"

The pilot looked down at Nate. "Hullo there. I must say, you're the youngest pilot I've seen here."

"Oh, I'm not a pilot, actually." Too late, Nate saw the twinkle in the man's eye and realized he'd been teasing.

Embarrassed and afraid he'd lose his nerve, Nate blurted out, "I was wondering if you have room for a passenger when you return to England?"

The pilot thought a moment. "I suppose I will. Don't think there'll be *that* much mail."

There was a rustle of movement at Nate's back, then a sniffing sound. The pilot's gaze zeroed in on Nate's shoulder, and he frowned. "I'd be happy to take *you*, mate, but not that. No gremlins on my plane."

Nate's hopes, which had begun to soar, dropped like a stone.

"But if you leave it behind, you're welcome to come along. I'll take off again at noon. Meet me back here then. Alone," he said pointedly.

"Thank you," Nate mumbled, then turned around to head back to their quarters.

"So, are yous going to leave me here?" Greasle asked, sounding surprisingly cheerful.

"I can't," Nate said glumly.

"I wouldn't mind, you know." The gremlin crawled all the way out of the pack and perched herself on Nate's shoulder.

"There'd be lots for me to eats." She looked around at the nearby planes and licked her lips.

"I know," Nate said. "And Aunt Phil would be furious with me. You heard what she said—I'm supposed to keep you away from the planes, not turn you loose on them."

"Oh." Greasle's disappointment stung. Nate had thought they were friends. It was disheartening to learn she'd turn him aside for a bit of grease and oil.

Discouraged, Nate headed for their tent. The only good thing was that Aunt Phil didn't know about his failed plan. He was grateful for that much, at least. With nothing else to do, Nate opened his rucksack to take out his sketchpad. His hand bumped into something round and hard.

The phoenix egg.

He lifted the treasure from his pack and carefully unwrapped the handkerchief that kept it from getting scratched or cracked. Both the egg and the handkerchief were coated in ash. The egg itself was about the size of his fist, and the colors of a deep sunset swirled in its depths. Just looking at it made Nate feel hopeful. He had succeeded with the phoenix. Surely he could take comfort in that. He set the egg down and began to draw.

MR. PICKLE

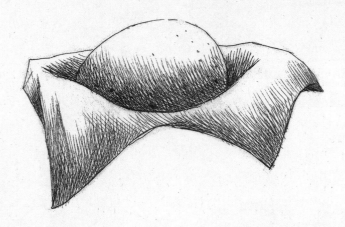

A short while later, a disturbance outside the tent interrupted his thoughts. He hastily rewrapped the egg. Just as he was storing it safely in his pack, Aunt Phil called out to him. "Nathaniel? Could you come out here for a moment please?"

"Uh-oh," Greasle said, crawling back into the pack. "Someone's in trouble."

Nate slowly opened the tent flap and peeked outside. Aunt Phil stood there with about half a dozen men, all of them looking angry. Nate swallowed. "Yes, Aunt Phil?"

She turned to him, her face no longer warm and friendly.

"That's him," a man yelled out, pointing. Nate recognized the pilot he'd asked for a ride. "He's the one with the gremlin."

An angry murmur went up from the small crowd. It was all Nate could do not to dive back into the tent and hide.

A mechanic in overalls with grease-stained hands stepped forward. "What's the big idea, bringing one o' them here?"

"Yeah!" Their voices grew louder.

"Gentlemen, gentlemen," Aunt Phil said. "If you'll give me a minute, I'll explain."

"There ain't no explanation, except you're daft," the mechanic said. "Now get on out of here before that critter attaches itself to one of our planes."

"I'm afraid we can't leave until our final crate arrives. However, as soon as it does—"

"I don't think you understand. You're leaving, or else." The mechanic brandished a large wrench at Aunt Phil.

She drew herself up to her full height. "You are sorely mistaken if you think for one moment we are going to be intimidated by the likes of you. Yes, the boy has a gremlin—"

Mutters sprang up anew.

"Think!" she said. "He is a beastologist-in-training. How

do you expect him to learn how to exterminate gremlins if he doesn't have any experience with them?"

Some of the angry looks gave way to thoughtful ones. Nate stared at Aunt Phil in surprise. Was that why she let him keep Greasle? Because she wanted to teach him how to exterminate gremlins?

"Could any of you have learned how to fly a plane if you'd never gotten near one?" She met each one of their eyes, and slowly their angry gazes dropped.

"Still would be a good idea for you to get on your way," someone muttered.

Just then, Mr. Pickle came lumbering in their direction lugging a large crate. Aunt Phil's face lit up. "Aha! There's our final delivery now. We'll be on our way at once, gentlemen." With those words, she grabbed Nate by the arm and dragged him back into their quarters, securing the tent flap firmly behind them.

She put her hands on her hips and glared at him. "I thought I told you to keep that thing out of sight?"

Nate squirmed under her furious gaze. "I tried to! Really. It's just that . . ."

"It's just what? Tell me while you pack because we are leaving here in precisely two minutes."

Grateful for the chance to look away, Nate began to blindly stuff things into his rucksack. Just how mad was she, he wondered? What would his punishment be? Whenever Miss Lumpton had gotten angry with him, she'd taken away one of his few privileges. One time, she'd even left him behind on their weekly trip to town.

Wait! He glanced up at Aunt Phil, who was lashing down the last of her packs. Maybe this could turn out all right after all. "I'm sorry I got us in trouble with all those men," he said. "But see," he rushed to add, "that's why you should leave me behind. I'm sure to make lots more mistakes. I warned you I wasn't very good at this travel and adventure stuff."

Aunt Phil laid the pack down on the cot. Her eyes were calmer now, and Nate found it a little easier to breathe. "Why are you so afraid of going to the Sudan?" she asked.

"'Scuse me?" Greasle poked her head out of Nate's pack. "Have you even read that stupid beastie book of yours? That thing is dangerous! We won'ts last one minute around that basil lick thing."

Aunt Phil glanced at Nate sharply and he thought she seemed mad again. "You consulted *The Book of Beasts*?"

Afraid to meet her gaze, he looked down at his feet. "Yes, ma'am. I'm sorry."

"Don't apologize! As the next beastologist, you have as much right to that book as anyone."

"I do?"

"Yes. I was only waiting for an opportunity to talk about the basilisk when there was more time to explain." She paused a moment, then continued. "There is nothing to be worried about, you know. You're merely to watch and learn this time around."

"Watch and learn," he repeated.

"Besides, you're the only other Fludd left. The only one who can be a beastologist after I'm gone. We've got to stay on top of your training or you'll never be ready."

Nate wasn't sure which was more upsetting: the thought of Aunt Phil passing away, or the responsibility for so many beasts falling on his shoulders. He wasn't exactly great with animals. Nor did he have any of the necessary Fludd skills that would make him a good adventurer. The phoenix had been one thing. It was beautiful and not life threatening in any way. The basilisk was something else altogether. Something dangerous and terrifying.

With these unhappy thoughts circling in his head like vultures, Nate followed Aunt Phil to the plane.

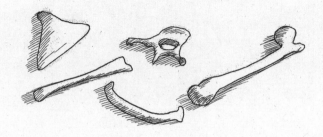

Chapter Five

THE CRATE MR. PICKLE HAD BEEN CARRYING now waited for them near the plane. Beady eyes peered out between the slats.

"What is that?" Nate asked Aunt Phil.

"Our secret weapon against the basilisk," she said, her voice cool.

The secret weapon threw itself against the side of the crate, wanting out. "But it's so small!" Nate said.

"Don't kid yourself, Nate. Small things can be danger-ous, under the right circumstances. Here, now, put this un-der your feet. It'll be a bit cramped, but there is simply no

room in the cargo area. Not with all the fuel."

Nate did not relish the idea of riding for twelve hours with his feet propped on something that could destroy the basilisk. He decided to try again. "If there isn't any room for me . . ."

"Nonsense." Aunt Phil's voice was brisk, but he didn't think there was any anger left in it. "There's plenty of room. Now, get in so we can take off."

Nate climbed into his seat and slipped his goggles on. He set his feet gingerly on top of the crate, then jerked them back at a sharp hissing sound. He sat with his knees pulled up next to his ears for two minutes before he realized he

couldn't fly across the entire Sahara like that. Slowly, he lowered his feet onto the crate again. This time, nothing happened. Even so, he was pretty sure he wouldn't relax until the flight was over.

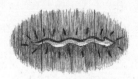

It was nearly dark when they drew in for a landing. Nate's head ached and his eyes burned. He'd spent the whole day squinting down, trying to find the faint lines of the furrows that would keep them on course. He'd been terrified that if he looked away—even for just a moment—they'd lose their way.

"Hold on!" Aunt Phil called out. "There's no landing strip here, so who knows how this old tub will handle it!"

Nate closed his eyes and gripped the sides of the plane. The jolt of the impact knocked his knees up into his chin. His teeth clacked together and he grunted as they bounced three more times, then hit a rock and bounced off to the side, before finally shuddering to a stop.

Greasle crept out of her hiding place, rubbing her elbow. "Someone needs to teach that old woman how to fly," she muttered.

"Shh!" Nate glanced nervously at Aunt Phil. That was all he needed—for her to overhear the gremlin criticizing her flying skills. Nate creaked to his feet, grabbed his pack, and threw one very stiff leg over the side, then the other.

"Excellent job navigating with the furrows, Nate," Aunt Phil said as she climbed awkwardly to the ground. "These old eyes of mine lost sight of them more than once, but you didn't. Good work. Now let's make camp."

Nate took in the desolate area around the plane. It would be another uncomfortable night.

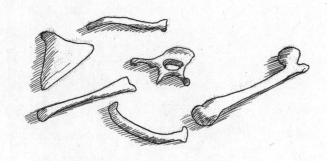

Chapter Six

EARLY THE NEXT MORNING, Nate found himself standing on the bank of a muddy brown river. "The Niger," Aunt Phil announced. "The very river Isidore Fludd sailed down nearly five hundred years ago."

Certainly the boat waiting for them looked as if it were the same one Isidore Fludd had used. It was nothing more than a rickety old canoe with a grass roof and a small motor. A man sat nearby, sipping from a metal flask. He had a dirty red scarf at his neck and his shirtsleeves rolled up. He hadn't shaved in days. He was exactly the kind of person

Nate's old governess, Miss Lumpton, would have crossed the street to avoid.

When the man saw them, he hastily shoved the flask into his pocket and rose to his feet. "Le doctor, I presume?"

Aunt Phil nodded her head and eyed him warily. "Phil Fludd. And you would be . . . ?"

"Jean-Claude LaFou. At your service. Me and *Queenie*, that is." He patted the canoe fondly.

Nate's heart sank as he realized *this* was the captain. A brief look of dismay passed over Aunt Phil's face as well, but she hid it quickly. "Excellent. You know the route, then?"

"Like the back of my hand. Get in and we'll shove off."

The next few minutes were spent trying to get everything into the canoe without tipping it over. Nate chose a spot as far away from Aunt Phil's mysterious crate as possible. The captain's assistant, Kwami, grabbed a pole and pushed them away from shore while the captain took a seat at the back of the boat. When he started up the motor, there was a furious rustling in Nate's pack. Greasle poked her head out, her big eyes zeroing in on the small engine.

Aunt Phil cleared her throat and sent Nate a warning glance.

"Be good, now," Nate reminded the gremlin.

"Me's always good. But I smells lovely, tasty oil." She stared longingly at the loud, clattering engine.

"*Sacre bleu!*" Jean-Claude said. "What is *that?*"

Kwami spoke rapidly, gesturing with the hand that wasn't holding the river pole. Jean-Claude shook his head. "*Non.* That is no monkey." He rubbed his eyes and peered at it again. "*Le petite* gargoyle, perhaps?"

"It's a gremlin," Nate explained.

"A grem-leen? Never heard of such a thing." With his eyes still on Greasle, Jean-Claude's free hand reached into his pocket for the flask. He took a quick sip, then replaced it, still eyeing Greasle warily.

The boat moved sluggishly through the silt-laden water. Nothing but sunbaked earth was visible as far as the eye could see. The heat of the early morning sun burned through Nate's shirt, and he could feel prickles of sweat begin to form. He was glad for the hat that protected his head. The motor droned on, sounding like an angry hummingbird. Kwami's pole dipped and splashed in the river as he steered them. Nate's eyes drifted shut and his head dropped to his chest.

"Nate!" He snapped awake to find Aunt Phil glaring at Greasle, who was slinking toward the motor.

He reached out and pulled the gremlin back. "Stop it!"

he hissed. Didn't she realize she was on thin ice with Aunt Phil?

Kwami's excited shout interrupted his scolding. Nate's mouth snapped shut as Jean-Claude leaped to his feet and grabbed a rifle from under his seat. Up ahead, Nate saw the river boiling and churning. His heart sank. Rapids? A waterfall?

"What is it?" Aunt Phil got to her feet, too, making the canoe wobble.

"Crocodiles," Jean-Claude spat.

As they drew closer, Nate could make out the huge, long bodies and gaping jaws of a dozen crocodiles. There was a loud click behind him. Nate turned to find Jean-Claude taking aim with his rifle.

Before he could pull the trigger, Aunt Phil reached out and knocked the barrel aside so the shot went wide. "Stop that nonsense!" she said. "I am a beastologist, sir, and I will not stand idly by while you murder helpless animals."

"Crocodiles? Helpless?" Jean-Claude said.

"We can fend them off in other ways," Aunt Phil said rather primly. Then she turned to Kwami. "Are there more poles?"

He pointed to the bottom of the boat, where two other poles lay. "Excellent." She picked one up and handed it to Nate, then took the second one for herself. "Well, put your gremlin away and stand up," she told him. "We've work to do."

"Don't worry, I'm goin'," Greasle said. "Don't want to watch this anyway," she muttered, burrowing back into Nate's rucksack.

Using the pole to help balance himself, Nate slowly rose to his feet.

"You take the port side; I'll take starboard," Aunt Phil ordered.

Nate had no idea which side was which. He waited until she took up position on the right side, then he took up position on the left. Crocodiles surrounded the boat. Their sinister eyes peered up at him from the water's surface.

"Ready, now," Aunt Phil said.

"What exactly am I supposed to do?" Nate asked, trying not to panic.

"Just poke at them a bit and try to get them to stay back."

He stared at the spindly pole in his hand, then at the enormous crocodile in front of him. *Is she kidding?*

There was a quiet sound of metal sliding against metal behind him.

"Stop!" Aunt Phil yelled.

Jean-Claude had picked up his rifle again.

"If you touch that one more time, I will strike you." She brandished her pole at him. "Do you understand?"

"*Sacre bleu,*" he muttered, placing the rifle back on the floor of the boat.

"Your job is to steer us out of here as quickly as possible. Got it?"

"Got it," he said. He started to reach for his flask, stopping when an ear-pounding bellow filled the air and the lead croc launched himself at their small boat.

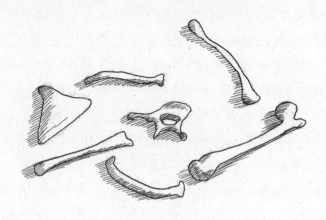

Chapter Seven

"Shoo!" Aunt Phil said, jabbing her pole at the crocodile. "Shoo!"

Kwami studied her for a moment, then copied her movement. "Shoo!" he repeated, poking at the two crocs that were blocking the boat.

Nate hoped Aunt Phil knew what she was doing. He gripped his pole tighter and thrust it toward the nearest crocodile, surprised when it connected solidly with the animal's snout. "Shoo!" he said.

Startled by the jab, the croc paused, giving the boat a little room to maneuver by. After a few more jabs, the animals became fed up and backed away from the boat.

"It worked!" Nate said as he watched the crocodiles eye them warily.

"Of course it worked," Aunt Phil said, wiping her brow.

"*Of course it worked*," Jean-Claude mimicked in a tiny singsong voice. Nate shot him an annoyed glance, freezing when he saw Greasle crouched at his feet, her mouth open to catch the oil leaking from the small motor.

Nate dropped his pole and snatched Greasle away from the engine before Aunt Phil could see. "Stop it," he hissed, giving her a tiny shake.

Her ears drooped. "But I was just catching the drips, see? I wasn't taking any that was needed. It's not my fault the wee engine leaks."

Nate glanced over at Aunt Phil, but she was too busy talking to Kwami to have seen. "It's back into the pack for you," he told her firmly.

"Nate," Aunt Phil said just then, startling him. "Come here. And bring your rucksack."

Nate did as she'd said.

"It seems to me it would be helpful if you understood the nature of the sacred contract that binds the Dhughani, the Fludds, and basilisks together. Now, sit close, because I don't want Jean-Claude to learn of the basilisk or get any whiff of its location. I don't trust that man and his gun."

Nate settled himself on the bottom of the canoe and hoped he'd learn something reassuring.

"In the fifteenth century, one of Mungo Fludd's sons, Isidore, attended Prince Henry of Portugal's School of Navigation. Once he'd completed his studies, he hired himself aboard a ship. The ship had been ordered by Prince Henry to cross the Sea of Darkness—a rough, mysterious patch of ocean along the coast of Africa. It was said to contain strange beasts and untold dangers. Rumor had it that no men had ever sailed through it and survived. But Isidore's ship did. Not only that, they reached a trading post at the mouth of the Gambia River. Isidore decided to leave the ship and explore the African continent for a while. He traveled up the Gambia until he found the Niger River, the first European to do so. He even made it to the fabled land of Timbuktu, where he met Sunni Ali, the king of the Songhay Empire.

"At first, they were not happy to see this stranger in their land. But Sunni Ali was cunning and offered Isidore a deal. If Isidore could help them solve a particular problem, not only would he let Isidore live, but he and his family would be welcome by the Songhay people for all eternity.

"The problem turned out to be a basilisk, and Isidore *was* able to help them."

"Was it the same basilisk we're going after?" Nate asked.

"No, Nate. There have been many basilisks over the centuries. When Isidore Fludd returned to Europe two years later, his tales of African discovery became legend. However, the scribe who copied his diaries made an error in translation. That error sent generations of explorers to Timbuktu in search of a 'brilliant treasure,' when, in fact, Isidore had written of a 'shimmering wonder' of the African world whose brilliance scarred a man's eyes. That was, of course, the basilisk.

"More than a hundred years later, Isidore's great-grandson, Florian Fludd, returned to the Songhay Empire in his role as a beastologist. No one had seen a basilisk in all that time, and Florian wanted to follow up the initial contact. The Songhay people were true to their promise and

welcomed him warmly. During his visit, the Songhay Empire was overrun by Moroccans bearing guns—something the Songhay had no defense against—the empire began to crumble. However, with Florian's help, a small group of the Songhay retreated to these cliffs and holed up there.

With the cliffs at their back and the basilisks' greatly feared powers, they were safe from attack. Because the basilisk helped protect them from marauders, the Songhay entered into a sacred contract with the beast—they would take care of it and bring it offerings when there were no marauders for it to eat.

"Which is how the Dhughani, descendants of the original Songhay Empire, have come to care for the basilisks all these centuries."

The sun had begun to set by the time Aunt Phil finished her story. Nate spent the last hour of daylight sketching until Jean-Claude steered the boat toward the shore. Kwami used his pole to pull them all the way up on the bank so

they wouldn't float away during the night. Dinner was beans, straight out of the tin, and then they all spread out on the floor of the boat under thin blankets.

Nate was exhausted and thought sleep would come easily—that was before mosquitoes the size of grasshoppers came out in droves. They swarmed around his head, sounding for all the world like Aunt Phil's plane.

Finally, in desperation, he called Greasle over. "Can you do something about these things?" he asked, swatting one away from his face.

She shrugged, and Nate could see she was still pouting from her earlier scolding. He glanced over at the others, who all seemed to be sleeping soundly. "I'll make you a deal," he said. "I'll let you go lick all the oil drips—but only the drips—if you'll come back here and swat these mosquitoes away while I sleep."

Greasle's little face brightened. "You means it?"

"Yes," Nate said. He waited while she scampered over and licked up every last drip of oil from the engine. Then she hurried back over and settled herself near Nate's head. Hoping to finally catch a bit of sleep, Nate closed his eyes. He could still hear the droning of the mosquitoes, but it

was fainter as Greasle swatted them away from his head.
Then, suddenly, the droning stopped.

Nate opened his eyes to find Greasle chewing. "Not
bad," she told him. She reached up and snatched another
one out of the air. With a gleam in her eye, she dipped the
captured mosquito into a newly formed drop of oil on the
motor, then took a bite. "But even better with oil."

Shuddering in disgust, Nate pulled the blanket up over
his head and stuffed his fingers into his ears.

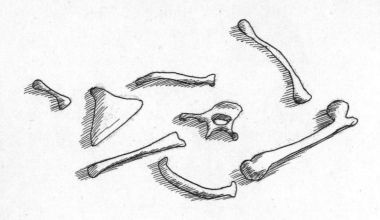

Chapter Eight

THE NEXT MORNING, Nate noticed that the river captain was sporting two large mosquito bites on his face and neck. Aunt Phil also had a couple. Everyone except him, it seemed. He made sure to give Greasle a big chunk of his breakfast for helping him.

They hadn't been under way for more than half an hour when the engine coughed and spluttered to a stop. Jean-Claude muttered something under his breath as he went to see what the problem was.

A moment later, Jean-Claude threw down the rag he was

holding in his hand. *"Sacre bleu!* The engine leaks. She is out of oil."

Kwami set his pole down and inched toward the back of the boat, where he and Jean-Claude began talking rapidly.

Aunt Phil gave Nate a hard, searching look and motioned him over. Nate gulped, then got to his feet and made his way to where she was sitting. "Is there something you wish to tell me, Nathaniel?"

"No, ma'am."

"Something about your gremlin getting at the engine, perhaps?"

Guilt flooded Nate's whole body. "I told her she could lick the drips, but that's all."

Aunt Phil put her hands on her hips. "How do you know she didn't create the leak in the first place? That's what gremlins do—*destroy* engines."

"B-because she promised she wouldn't," Nate said. He felt a movement at his feet and saw Greasle down there, staring up at Aunt Phil.

"I didn't break no engine," she said in her tiny voice. "I keeps my promises."

Aunt Phil sniffed. "So say you. Nate, put her in your

rucksack and see that she does not come out again. I'll decide what to do about her later."

His shoulders slumping, Nate scooped up Greasle. "Sorry," he whispered, then slipped her into the rucksack and buckled the straps shut.

"Well, we are stuck," Jean-Claude announced.

"Surely you have some extra oil on the boat?" Aunt Phil asked.

"*Non*, we do not *have some extra oil on the boat*," he mimicked. "It wasn't leaking before." Kwami gave him an odd look, one that made Nate suspect Jean-Claude was lying.

"We'll have to use the poles."

"But that will take ages!" Aunt Phil protested.

"*Oui*," Jean-Claude said curtly. "And if we want to arrive before nightfall, we best get started."

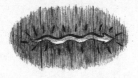

Nate spent the rest of the journey huddled miserably in his seat. When the sun was low in the sky, the captain finally turned the boat to shore. There was nothing but dirt and two barren thorn trees for as far as he could see. "Why are we stopping?" Nate asked.

"We're here," Aunt Phil said.

"Here?" Nate looked again to be sure he hadn't missed something.

"See those sandstone cliffs?" She pointed to the far distance, where Nate could just make out some tall, rocky cliffs. "That's where we're going."

As Nate stepped out of the boat, he saw a lone figure with three donkeys sitting under one of the thorn trees. The man lifted his hand in greeting. Nate waved back. "Who is that?" he asked Aunt Phil.

"Our guide," she said, lifting the mysterious crate out of the boat.

Once everything was unloaded, Kwami and Jean-Claude had a small argument over what to do next. They finally agreed that Kwami would hike out for the necessary supplies to fix the engine. He assured them he could be there and back in three days, which was exactly when Aunt Phil planned on returning.

Aunt Phil and Nate left the captain grumbling and made their way over to their guide. The ancient man's skin was as dark as midnight, and he had bristly white hair and a beard. He bowed respectfully before Aunt Phil. "I am Atanu," he said. "Servant to the Dolon. I was afraid you would not make it today after all."

Aunt Phil bowed back. "I'm sorry we were delayed." She sent Nate's backpack a disgruntled look.

"What's a Dolon?" Nate asked, relieved the man spoke English.

"The Dhughani's spiritual leader," Aunt Phil whispered back.

"If you are ready, I will take you to our village, Dr. Fludd."

They spent the next few minutes loading their gear and supplies onto the three donkeys. Aunt Phil gave Nate a boost so he could mount his. It was much more comfortable than the camel, he thought, but just as stubborn. *"Hut hut hut,"* he said, slapping the reins. "Come on. Go." He dug his heels into the donkey's round, thick sides. With an annoyed bray, the donkey broke into a teeth-rattling trot just long enough to catch up with Aunt Phil and Atanu.

As they left the Niger River behind, the harsh red cliffs ahead grew larger, their sharp edges jutting against the skyline. They reminded Nate of the crocodiles' teeth and his fingers itched to sketch them.

Near the base of the cliffs, they came upon a deserted village. There was no sign of people. No birds sang; no roosters crowed. There weren't even any flies buzzing around. The few scrub trees were scorched, their branches gnarled and brown. Piles of rubble littered the ground. The grass huts were so brown and twisted, it looked as if a strong wind would turn them to ash. A horrible stench hung in the air.

"Best cover your face with this, Nate." Aunt Phil held out a thick scarf. "It's hard to know how much of the basilisk's venom still lingers."

Despite the sweltering heat, Nate took the scarf and wrapped it twice around his mouth and nose.

"The basilisk came through here two days ago," Atanu told them. "Luckily, the villagers escaped unharmed."

Nate could only hope that he and Aunt Phil would be so lucky.

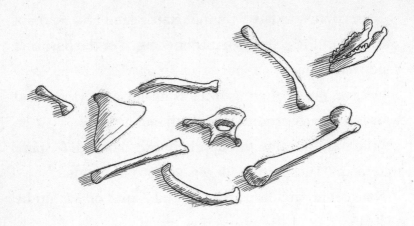

Chapter Nine

THE SETTING SUN WASHED THE CLIFFS in a warm red light, making them look like they were on fire. Strange spires and rooftops sprouted out of the bluffs. It wasn't until they were closer that Nate realized the village was actually built into the rock face itself.

The donkeys made their sure-footed way up a winding path through the lower ridges until they arrived at the village. The houses were made entirely of mud except for the pointed grass roofs they wore like jaunty hats.

When their small group reached the village square, people came out to greet them. Their faces were friendly and welcoming. The crowd parted to let an old man in white robes and a red bonnet approach. As he drew closer, Nate spied an enormous pearl nestled in his armband.

Aunt Phil bowed to the man, but waited for him to speak first.

The man bowed back. "I bring you greetings, Dr. Fludd, and I thank you for coming. How is your health?"

"Greetings, Dolon," Aunt Phil answered. "My health is very good, thank you."

"And how is your family?" he asked.

"Very good" was Aunt Phil's reply. Nate looked at her in surprise. Her only family other than him had been lost at sea, which did not seem *very good* to him.

"And how is your health, Dolon?" she asked.

"Very good." The old man's eyes sparkled in approval. "You greet like a true Dhughani."

Aunt Phil smiled and bowed again. "My nephew and I thank you for inviting us to your village."

The old man studied Nate. "Is he to be the next beastologist, then?"

"Yes," Aunt Phil. "His name is Nathaniel."

Not sure what he was supposed to do, Nate bowed. "Pleased to meet you. Sir."

"And I you," said the Dolon. "He is the same age as when you and I first met, yes?" he asked Aunt Phil.

"Close," she said.

"I wonder if you told him the story of our first meeting?"

Nate couldn't be sure, but it looked like Aunt Phil was blushing. "No, I haven't."

The Dolon looked back at Nate. "She was twelve years

old and had come with her Uncle Seymour, who was the beastologist back then."

Aunt Phil interrupted. "I'm sure he doesn't want to hear this old story."

"Oh, but I am sure he would enjoy it." The Dolon winked at Nate, as if they were sharing some private joke. He leaned in closer. "Your aunt spent the entire visit trying to look under the basilisk's tail!"

Aunt Phil's cheeks were bright red now.

"She was trying to see if it was a boy or a girl!" the Dolon explained. Then he laughed, a rich, rolling sound that seemed to echo off the cliffs above them. Nate found himself smiling back. The Dolon had been right. Nate did enjoy the story.

"Now, come," the Dolon said, wiping the laughter from his eyes. "Do you wish to get settled first, or eat and hear of the basilisk's escape?"

Just then, Nate's stomach growled loudly.

Aunt Phil smiled at him. "Eat, I think."

The Dolon led them to a smaller square and told them to have a seat. Nate started to sit on a pile of stones in the center, but Aunt Phil grabbed his arm and pulled him away. "We can't sit there. It's a sacred place."

Embarrassed, Nate muttered, "Sorry," then sat on the hard-packed dirt next to Aunt Phil. The entire village had followed them and settled down to watch. Two of the women came forward, carrying food. One of them smiled and handed him a bowl. Except it wasn't really a bowl.

"It's a gourd," Aunt Phil explained when she saw him staring at it. "They dry them and use them for food and drink."

Inside was some yellow mushy stuff that looked like a kind of porridge. Chunks of meat floated in it.

Nate glanced at Aunt Phil, who lifted her gourd to her mouth. Nate did the same. It wasn't bad. The porridge tasted like nutty rice. He took another mouthful, this time getting a piece of the meat.

He bit into it, his tongue curling as the smooth, pasty texture burst into his mouth. *Liver*. It was all he could do to keep from gagging. Miss Lumpton had forced him to eat liver once and he'd ended up being sick all over the dining room table. He desperately hoped he wouldn't be sick here. Not with the entire village watching.

He forced himself to swallow, then took a quick mouthful of porridge, hoping to erase the taste and texture from his mouth.

Just then, one of the Dhughani pointed at him and *oohed*. Nate froze. Could the man tell he hated liver? He glanced over at Aunt Phil, looking for a clue.

"It's your gremlin," she told him quietly. "She's decided to come out of her hidey-hole."

Greasle crept out of his rucksack. "Hungry," she said, petting his knee.

"Can I share with her?" Nate asked.

"If you like."

Nate fished a chunk of liver out and handed it to Greasle. If she thought mosquitoes were tasty, she'd probably love liver.

She popped it into her mouth. "Yum," she said, and smiled.

Perfect, Nate thought. As Aunt Phil and the Dolon talked, Nate cheerfully fed every last bit of liver to his gremlin.

"Our story begins five days ago," the Dolon said. "When the basilisk did not come for his nightly feeding. This happens sometimes, so we were not duly concerned. Except he did not come for a second night, either. That has never happened."

"Had he been feeding regularly up until that point?" Aunt Phil asked.

The Dolon nodded. "The next day, we mounted a party to enter his sacred caves. We found them empty."

"This is a puzzle, to be sure. However, I won't be able to do anything until I see his lair." She glanced up at the dark sky. "We will have to wait to enter his caves until first thing in the morning," Aunt Phil said.

Nate groaned to himself. Why did it have to be caves? Caves meant bats.

He hated bats.

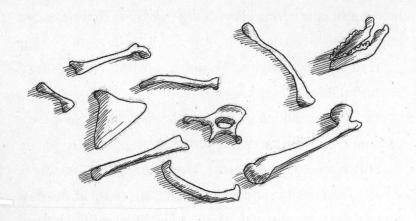

Chapter Ten

IN THE MORNING, after another bowl of porridge—which Nate found out was actually boiled millet—Aunt Phil, the Dolon, and Nate set off for the basilisk's cave. Greasle was curled up asleep inside Nate's rucksack. Probably still trying to digest all that liver she'd eaten.

"That is where we must go," the Dolon said. He pointed—up, up, up—to a small hollow in the cliff side.

Nate had to tilt his head all the way back just to see it. "How do we get up there?"

"We climb," the Dolon said.

Nate looked at the sheer cliff face, then back at the Dolon. Maybe this was a joke, kind of like his story about Aunt Phil. "You're teasing, aren't you—hey! Wait for me!" While he had stood gawking, Aunt Phil and the Dolon had started to climb. Nate scrambled to catch up.

The climb was the hardest thing Nate had ever done. Parts of the cliff didn't have any footholds or handholds, or at least none that he could see. Not until Aunt Phil pointed them out. Even worse, the Dolon and his aunt could climb like mountain goats. Nate felt gawky and clumsy next to them.

Nate was hot and sweaty, his fingers raw. He had to force himself to keep from looking down. His mind kept wondering what it would feel like to go *splat*.

The final leg of the climb was the worst.

There was a giant chasm, much too wide to jump across. A rickety, handmade ladder had been laid over the gap, like a bridge. The Dolon scrambled across, then Aunt Phil. Nate grabbed the ladder, biting back a shout as it wobbled and nearly sent him tumbling into the yawning abyss below.

"Come on, Nate! You can do it," Aunt Phil called to him. "Just don't look down."

"Then how am I supposed to know where to put my feet?" he called back.

"By feel."

By feel? The only thing he could *feel* was the fear racing through him like a runaway train. With no other choice, he took a deep breath, looked away from his feet, and clambered across the ladder as quickly as he could, hoping he'd make it across before the whole thing fell apart.

Sweat was pouring down his face when he finally reached the other side. It was all he could do to keep from kissing the ground beneath his knees.

As they drew closer to the cliff face, Nate's heart stuttered in his chest. It was decorated with animal skins and skulls. In the middle of all that sat a thick, crooked door made of rough wood. A snake was carved into its surface. Nate tried to swallow, but his throat was as dry as one of the bones hanging in front of him. He desperately wanted to know why they were there, but was afraid to ask.

Aunt Phil bent to examine the door. "It didn't get out this way, did it?"

"We do not know."

Aunt Phil pulled her scarf up to cover her mouth and

nose. The Dolon covered his face, then unlocked the heavy iron lock that barred the wooden door. It creaked open to reveal a gaping black hole.

"Maybe I should wait out here for you?" Nate suggested hopefully.

"No, Nate." Aunt Phil gave him a gentle shove forward. He quickly yanked his scarf into place as he stumbled into the cave. The air was stale and musty with an underlying sickly sweet smell.

The Dolon lit a torch in the wall, then handed it to Aunt Phil. She waved it away. "No, I've got a flashlight here," she said, pulling one from her heavy pack. When she turned it on, the light flared along the cave walls. Nate gasped and took a step closer to her.

Hundreds more skulls had been set into the walls. Empty eye sockets gaped back at him. Some had large facial bones—like a baboon. Others sported the long sharp beak of some sort of bird with a pair of spindly feet dangling below. Nate's own feet were itching to turn tail and run all the way back to the village. He wondered why the bones were there. A warning, maybe?

Almost as if sensing his question, Aunt Phil spoke softly into his ear. "It is the Dhughani's way of honoring those animals sacrificed to the basilisk," she explained.

Some honor, Nate thought, but kept to himself.

"You've got a flashlight in your pack, too, Nate," Aunt Phil said. "Why don't you get it out?"

Nate opened the outside pocket of his rucksack and retrieved his. He turned it on, feeling a little better with something solid and light-generating in his hand.

A half dozen smaller caverns opened up off the main

cave. "Um, what exactly are we looking for?" he asked, trying to pretend his heart wasn't about to gallop out of his chest.

"Anything that might tell us how the basilisk escaped," Aunt Phil said. "A hole in the cave wall, an opening from above, signs of a landslide or cave-in. Even a small pool that might lead to an underground stream that it could have followed out. We should split up for greatest efficiency."

"Since I'm just supposed to watch and learn, shouldn't I stay with you?" Nate asked.

"The basilisk isn't here, Nate." Aunt Phil's voice was gentle. "There's nothing to be afraid of."

"What if it returns?" Nate asked.

"Then we would be lying sick on the ground even now, gasping for fresh air."

"Oh." He could tell she had meant that to be comforting.

The Dolon thrust two balls of rough red twine at them. "The caverns are deep and twisting and it is easy to lose your path. Take these so that you may find your way back. Unwind the string as you go. It will mark your return so you don't get lost."

Nate and Aunt Phil took their balls of twine from the Dolon. "Well," Aunt Phil said, "see you all back here in a bit. Holler if you find anything."

As Nate watched the others disappear from sight, he had to fight the urge to run after them. The empty skulls in the wall stared at him, making his skin crawl. He didn't want to be alone in this place.

But wait! He wasn't alone. He swung his pack off his shoulders, yanked it open, and peered inside. "Do you want out?" he asked Greasle, hoping very much that she did.

The gremlin's head emerged cautiously. "I don't know. Does I?" She looked at the eerie skulls, then squealed and ducked back inside. "Maybe I'll just stay in here," she called back to him.

Nate reached into the pack and snagged her. "Oh no you don't. I could use an extra pair of eyes." He ripped a small corner of his scarf off and helped her pull it up over her mouth and nose. Then he carefully set her on the ground. "Ready?" he asked.

She folded her arms and glared at him.

"Come on," he said. "Let's just get this over with."

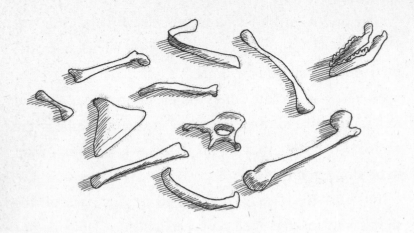

Chapter Eleven

O*NCE THEY WERE AWAY FROM THE WALL OF SKULLS*, Greasle didn't seem to be bothered by the dark at all. She scampered easily from boulder to crevice. Nate clutched his flashlight tighter and wished he were more like the gremlin. She didn't have a scared bone in her body. Well, except when it came to Aunt Phil—Greasle was plenty scared of her.

Nate swept the light beam against the cavern walls. The truth was, he had no idea what he was looking for. A method of escape, Aunt Phil had said. It seemed to Nate

that he needed to know a lot more about the basilisk to understand how it could have gotten loose.

He shone his flashlight behind him, relieved to see the trail of red string pointing the way back. Turning back around, he swept the light in an arc. It caught something on the floor of the cave. Something that glittered.

It looked like—jewels?

He squatted down and shone the light directly on them. They glittered blue, green, and red and looked like fish scales. Basilisk scales? *The Book of Beasts* had said they were valuable, but he hesitated. Everything about the basilisk was poisonous—its breath, its gaze. Its scales were probably poisonous, too. Even so, Nate's fingers itched to pick them up. It seemed like something a beastologist ought to do—collect samples. He had a phoenix egg. Basilisk scales would round out his collection nicely.

He set the flashlight on the ground, then fished a handkerchief out of his pocket. Careful not to let his skin touch the brightly colored scales, he picked them up and wrapped them in the handkerchief.

Greasle appeared at his knee. "Whatcha got there?"

"Basilisk scales," Nate said.

"Pretty." Greasle reached out to touch one and Nate jerked them away from her.

"No!" He stood up, trying to keep the scales out of her reach.

Before he could explain about the poison, Greasle made a face at him. "I wants to find some jools of my own," she said. And with that, the gremlin scampered down a cavern to the right.

"No, Greasle! Come back!" Nate swung the flashlight on her just in time to see her disappear down the tunnel. That dumb gremlin! He should just let her go. See how she liked being all alone in this creepy place. Except then he'd be all alone, too. And what if she found more scales and got poisoned? She *was* his responsibility.

Nate poked his head into the tunnel Greasle had taken. "Come back here, Greasle!" He flashed his light into the darkness. There was no sign of her.

Grumbling to himself, he scrunched down and took a few more steps. "Greasle?" he whispered. Still no answer.

He checked his ball of red twine and saw there was plenty of string left. He got down on his hands and knees and began to crawl after her.

The cavern was small and narrow and went on forever. No matter how many times Nate called after Greasle, she never answered. He couldn't help wondering what would happen if the basilisk came back. Nate's heart started to beat too fast and it felt as if he couldn't get enough oxygen. He wanted to rip the scarf from his face, but of course he couldn't. Not with the basilisk's venom hanging in the air.

"Greasle?" he called again.

When he rounded the next bend in the cavern, he blinked. It was lighter, and he could feel the faint stirring of a fresh breeze on his face. At the next turn, he had to shut his eyes against the bright light spilling into the cave. Once his eyes had adjusted, he saw that he was able to stand up. He rose to his feet and looked around. It appeared to be the basilisk's den. The sickly sweet stench of the basilisk's poisonous fumes was stronger, and piles of old bones were everywhere. Its scales, glittering like precious gems, littered the floor. Nate was glad he'd found them before—

"Greasle! Where are you?" he called.

"Here." She poked her head out from behind a skull the size of his rucksack.

She was dangerously close to the scales. "Get away from there!"

Ignoring him, the gremlin reached for a large, shiny green scale.

"Don't touch it!" he called out. "It might be poisonous!"

Greasle jerked her hand away as if she'd been burned. "Nasty scales," she said.

"Yes, but valuable, according to *The Book of Beasts*." Nate hurried over and scooped her onto his shoulder. He was hot and sweaty from crawling through the tunnel, and the cool air on his back felt good. He turned and saw a gaping hole in the wall. It looked new. Large chunks of stone had been hewn from the side of the cliff, creating a passage to the outside. There were harsh white scrapes and cut marks on the red sandstone. He was pretty sure this was what Aunt Phil had meant by a method of escape. His heart started to race. Why did he have to be the one to find it?

Slowly he approached the opening. What if the basilisk was waiting outside? He cautiously poked his head out, ready to leap back into the safety of the cave if necessary.

Nothing moved. He lifted his foot to step outside, but it

caught on something hard and he tripped. A loud clatter and clang echoed back into the cave. Nate looked down at his feet.

A pick and an ax lay on the ground in front of him. He looked back at the opening, realization dawning.

The basilisk hadn't escaped. Someone had dug it out.

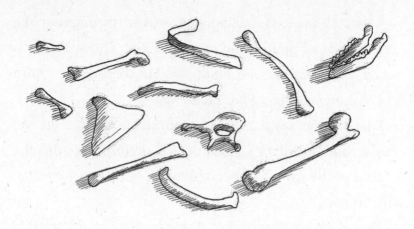

Chapter Twelve

"WE'VE GOT TO FIND AUNT PHIL." Nate snagged Greasle and put her into the rucksack. He turned around and raced back through the narrow tunnel, his heart thudding against his ribs. It seemed to take forever. When he finally reached the main cavern, there was no sign of Aunt Phil or the Dolon. They were both still out searching the rest of the caverns.

Nate stepped into the tunnel that Aunt Phil had taken. He cupped one hand around his mouth and called, "Aunt Phil!"

Aunt Phil, Aunt Phil, Aunt Phil echoed throughout the caves, reaching up into the soaring ceiling above. Nate listened, but there was no response. He tried again. "Aunt Phil!" *Aunt Phil, Aunt Phil, Aunt Phil.*

This time he heard a rushing sound. He glanced up and saw a thousand dark shapes detach themselves from the ceiling of the cave. In his excitement, Nate had forgotten all about—

"Bats!" he whispered. He threw himself to the ground and clapped his arms over his head as a thousand winged creatures swooped down on him.

When Aunt Phil arrived fifteen minutes later, that's how she found him—still plastered to the floor, afraid to move. "Nate?" she called as she crouched at his side.

He lifted his head and peered up at the ceiling. "Are they gone?"

"Are who gone?"

"The bats," he whispered.

Aunt Phil's face relaxed. "Yes, they've all gone." Then she held out a hand and helped him to his feet. "Is that why you were calling me?"

"No! I found something. I think it's the way the basilisk escaped."

Just then the Dolon appeared in the far tunnel. "I heard shouting," he said.

"Nate thinks he's found the escape route," Aunt Phil explained. Nate was grateful she kept the bat incident to herself. "Lead the way," she told him.

Luckily, Nate had thought to leave his string in place to guide them back to the hole. If not, he could never have found it again. Aunt Phil and the Dolon had to crouch down very low to get through the small crawlspace. He heard their grunts and muttering behind him. "It's not much farther," he told them.

Finally the narrow passage opened up and revealed the basilisk's lair. Aunt Phil and the Dolon blinked, and then Aunt Phil hurried over to the gaping hole in the cave wall. She bent to inspect it.

"There's a pick and an ax outside," Nate said.

Aunt Phil and the Dolon exchanged worried glances, then went out to see. "Someone set it free on purpose," Aunt Phil said, examining the tools.

Nate cleared his throat. "Greasle was the one who discovered it." He wanted to remind Aunt Phil that the gremlin could be useful.

Aunt Phil merely raised an eyebrow before addressing the Dolon. "Do you have any enemies who would wish your people harm?"

The Dolon shrugged. "We have had many enemies over the centuries," he said. "But I do not know of any who would loose this upon the world."

As Aunt Phil and the Dolon continued to discuss the possibilities, Nate wandered away toward the edge of the outcropping. It was a sheer drop-off that made him dizzy when he looked down. He pulled his gaze back up, then frowned.

Before him, the Sahel stretched out for miles, as far as the eye could see. Cutting through the landscape was a wide brown swath. It looked almost like a . . . a path. A path of destruction, Nate realized. "Aunt Phil!" he called again.

"What is it?" she asked as she hurried over.

Nate pointed to the wide brown trail. "The basilisk," Aunt Phil said.

"The basilisk," the Dolon agreed.

"And we know where it's heading," Aunt Phil said grimly.

"We do?" Nate asked.

"Yes, look." She pointed to the winding path. "It's getting closer and closer to the river."

The Dolon looked ill. "And if it gets to the river . . ." His voice grew silent, as if he could not bring himself to say the words.

"It will poison the entire water supply all along the Niger," Aunt Phil said quietly. "All the animals who depend on it, the fish who swim in it, and the people who drink from it will be poisoned."

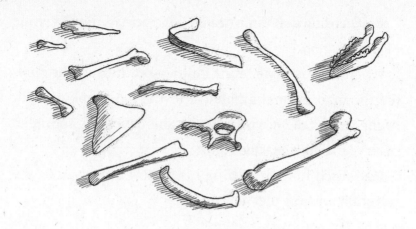

Chapter Thirteen

"DO YOU THINK YOU CAN SKETCH THAT FOR US?" Aunt Phil asked Nate. "A map of the basilisk's progress and where it might be heading?"

"Me?" Nate asked.

"Yes, you."

"I think so." Nate set down his rucksack and took out his sketchpad. He sat himself on a flat rock and began to draw, his pencil trembling slightly in his hand. It felt like the most important drawing he'd ever done.

As if sensing that importance, Greasle stayed quiet while he drew.

When he was done, Aunt Phil looked it over. She studied the map, then compared it to the landscape in front of them. "Excellent work, Nate." She patted his shoulder. "You've drawn it exactly."

He busied himself putting his sketchbook away so she wouldn't see how pleased he was.

"Well," Aunt Phil said, "I think we've learned all we can here. Let's get back to the village and start asking some questions."

When they got back to the village, the Dolon called all the Dhughani together. Nate took a seat on a rock and waited. When everyone was assembled, Aunt Phil spoke to the Dolon in a low voice. "I'm going to explain to them that someone freed the basilisk on purpose. Ask if there have been any strangers sighted near the village in the past few days." The Dolon nodded his agreement.

As Aunt Phil spoke to the Dhughani people in their tongue, Nate wondered if she expected him to learn all the languages that she knew.

When she had finished, the small crowd erupted in excited voices, everyone talking at once. When they had quieted, the Dolon translated for Nate. "No strangers have been seen in our village. But Golu says that his wife's cousin has taken on a job as a guide. Golu will go to that village and question the man."

"Excellent," Aunt Phil said. "And we need to send messengers to all the villages in the basilisk's path. Nate, may I have your map, please?"

"My map?" he squeaked.

"Yes, I want to show them the direction the basilisk is moving in."

Blushing, Nate pulled the sketchbook from his rucksack and handed it to Aunt Phil. He didn't think it was good enough to show to other people.

As she held the drawing up for the crowd to see, the villagers talked excitedly again. After a few minutes of discussion, three men set out to warn the nearby villages that were in harm's way.

"Well," Aunt Phil said, "I think that's all we can do for the time being. Nate, you and I have a number of preparations to make while we wait for the others to return." They excused themselves and went to their small hut.

"It will be dark in a couple of hours, so I don't think we'll be able to leave tonight. With any luck, Golu will return before we go to sleep." She rifled through her pack, drew out a large pouch, and held it up. "Rue," she announced, as if she were offering him gold. "Of course, nothing can protect against direct contact with the venom, but rue is the one plant that can neutralize the basilisk's poisonous gaze. We'll make a tea of it. I want you to drink as much as you possibly can."

If it would protect him from the basilisk, Nate would happily drink mud from the Niger River.

Aunt Phil built a small fire and set a pot on to boil. Next, she pulled two round mirrors out of her pack and handed one to Nate. "These are our weapons of last resort. If something happens and we cannot stop the basilisk from poisoning the entire water supply, we will use the mirrors."

Nate stared at the mirror, the size of a dinner plate, in his hand. It looked harmless to him. "What will they do?"

"They will reflect the basilisk's venomous gaze back at it and kill it." A long moment of silence followed as her words sank in. "However," she continued, "I'd rather not kill it if we don't have to. Which is why I've brought our secret weapons."

Nate perked up. Was he finally going to learn what was in that crate?

Aunt Phil dropped a handful of the rue leaves into the boiling water, then got up and went over to the crate. "Ready?" she asked with a twinkle in her eye.

"I think so," Nate said, bracing himself.

Aunt Phil undid the latch at the top of the crate and lifted the door. Two sleek, furry shapes exploded out, moving so quickly that Nate barely had a chance to see them. They had bright, curious eyes and darted frantically about the room, exploring every nook and cranny.

"Meet Sir Roland and Lady of Shallot, Sallie for short," Aunt Phil said.

"Ferrets?" Nate asked in surprise.

"No, weasels," Aunt Phil corrected. "The basilisk's deadliest enemy—the one thing on earth that can withstand its poisonous gaze from closer than twenty paces."

"B-but they're so cute," Nate said.

"It's important to remember every creature on earth has at least one enemy," Aunt Phil explained. "And not all of them are ferocious looking. Even cute things can be dangerous, Nate." She stood up and poured two mugs of rue tea, then handed one to him. "Even you," she added, ruffling his hair.

The affectionate gesture surprised him, but he decided he kind of liked it.

One of the weasels—Roland, Nate thought—galloped over to sniff his knee. Nate bent down and caught the weasel's eyes. Once he had its attention, he held his hand out for it to sniff. Only then did he reach out to pet it.

"Where did you learn to do that?" Aunt Phil asked.

"Do what?"

"Approach animals that way."

Worried, Nate asked, "Did I do it wrong?"

"No. You did it exactly right."

Nate shrugged. "It just makes sense." The truth was, he approached animals like he wished people would approach him. Well, except for the sniffing part.

After another quick turn around the hut, the weasel was back at his knee, practically climbing up into his lap to see what was in the mug. Nate laughed and petted the creature, trying to get it to settle down. "Curious things, aren't they?"

"Very," Aunt Phil said.

Nate felt a movement behind him and saw that Greasle had crawled out of the rucksack. She glared unhappily at the weasel. "What is that?" she asked.

At the sound of her voice, the weasels raced over to her. Frantic with curiosity and twice as big as she was, they sent her tumbling end over teakettle. "Help!" she squeaked. "Call 'em off! They're killing me!"

Nate lifted the two weasels off Greasle. "They're just being friendly." As he set the weasels down Aunt Phil whistled a short single note. The weasels forgot about him and the gremlin and galloped off to explore Aunt Phil.

"Huh." The gremlin dusted herself off. "Seems to me you've already got a friend," she said with a loud sniff.

Nate stared at her in surprise. Was she jealous? He gently picked Greasle up and set her on his shoulder. "They're just weasels," he told her softly. "Nothing near as special as a gremlin. And they'll never be my friend like you are."

Greasle's face grew pink with pleasure. "Really?"

"Really," Nate said.

"If you're so fond of that gremlin, you'd best have her drink some of the tea," Aunt Phil suggested.

"Okay." Nate had meant what he'd said—she *was* his best friend. He held his mug up to her. She sniffed, wrinkled her nose, then took a sip.

She spit it out. "Yuck."

"Drink it," Nate ordered. "It will protect you from the basilisk's poison."

Greasle made a face. "Why don't they have to drinks it?" she asked, pointing at the weasels.

"Because they eat the leaves instead." Aunt Phil set a small pile of leaves on the floor. The weasels scampered over and began nibbling at the rue.

Feeling better that they had to share in the nasty stuff, Greasle drank her tea.

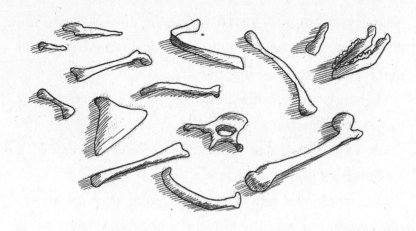

Chapter Fourteen

JUST AFTER DUSK, Golu returned, dragging his wife's cousin behind him. The man was nervous and afraid he was in trouble. Once the Dolon and Aunt Phil had assured him he wasn't, he began to talk. Aunt Phil translated quietly for Nate whenever the man paused for breath.

"Seven days ago," she explained, "a man came asking about the local rock formations. He claimed he was a geologist. The Dhughani led him up and down the cliffs. When they came too close to the basilisk's caverns, the guide steered the geologist away, but said nothing of the creature who lived there. He swears he did not reveal the Dhughani's sacred secret. They went back to the village that night, and in the morning, the stranger was gone."

There was a lot of murmuring as everyone digested this piece of information.

The Dolon looked at Aunt Phil. "He must have headed straight back to the basilisk."

"But wouldn't it have taken quite some time for him to dig through the rock?" Aunt Phil wondered. "That wall is thick. He had to have used explosives of some kind, dynamite or something. Wouldn't you have heard it?"

The Dolon looked chagrined. "Six nights ago, we *did* hear thunder, but assumed it was one of the rare storms moving through the area."

"That was it, then. He blasted the creature out." Aunt Phil grew furious. "Didn't he realize he could have harmed it?" She was so angry, she was shaking. Nate was pretty sure the stranger hadn't worried about hurting the basilisk. In fact, Nate was willing to bet that Aunt Phil was the only person in the world who'd worry about that.

She asked the guide a series of rapid questions. The man held his hand up to just below the top of Aunt Phil's head,

then held his arms apart, as if describing a barrel. Last, he pointed to Aunt Phil's hair, then Nate's.

She nodded politely and thanked him for his help. Then she turned to Nate. "Describe for me again the man you saw at the oasis in Arabia last week?"

"He was shorter than you, and round," Nate said. "And he had ginger-colored hair. Do you think they could be the same person?"

"It would be an amazing coincidence to run into two such men at two different places."

Nate thought for a moment. "But how did he get here before us? Wouldn't the mail service have said something if someone else had come through asking for that much fuel as well?"

Aunt Phil grew thoughtful. "Excellent point. And I think they would have, *if* he had used the British Mail Service. But there are other air facilities in Cairo. Not many, but a few. And he did have a head start on us."

Nate winced. That was his fault. If he had been better at navigating, they would have made it back to Wadi Rumba sooner and the stranger wouldn't have had such a lead. He waited for Aunt Phil to point that out, but much to his relief, she didn't.

The next morning, Aunt Phil woke Nate while it was still dark outside. She shoved another mug of rue tea into his hands and made him drink it. His stomach was so fluttery with nerves, he could hardly get it down. Today was the day he'd come face-to-face with the basilisk. The thought made him want to dive back into his bedroll.

"Make sure your mirror is well padded so it won't break on the ride," Aunt Phil told him as she secured her own pack.

Nate hoped he wouldn't have to use it. In fact, he secretly hoped they would never find the basilisk. He was pretty sure he could live his whole life happily without ever coming face-to-face with it.

But when he remembered all the people who were in danger, he felt ashamed. He was such a miserable coward. He didn't deserve the name Fludd.

As Nate reached into his rucksack to check on the mirror, Greasle tried to burrow deeper into the pack. Nate picked her up and plunked her on the ground next to his mug. "Time to drink more tea," he said, lifting the mug to her mouth.

Glaring at him, she glugged down a few swallows, then wiped her mouth. "There. Are you happy now?"

"Not happy, exactly," Nate said. "But I *am* glad you're protected against the poison."

The Dolon had their donkeys ready for them outside. He and Aunt Phil talked quietly as she secured her saddlebags on her mount. Nate tried to listen and could just barely make out what they said.

"Be careful," the Dolon told her as she climbed up on her donkey.

"Always," Aunt Phil replied.

Nate stared at her in surprise. He'd never met someone who was *less* careful than she was.

Then Aunt Phil slapped her reins and clicked her tongue,

and their donkeys took off at a trot. Bouncing atop her donkey, Aunt Phil compared Nate's map to her own.

"It looks to me like this village here, Dinka, is the last one standing between the basilisk and the river. We'll go there and try to head it off."

Nate tried not to let his mind dwell on what lay ahead of them. Aunt Phil knew what she was doing, he reassured himself. When at last a village appeared on the horizon, Nate swallowed nervously and asked, "Is that it?"

Aunt Phil consulted her map again. "No, that's Gando."

As they drew closer, Nate gagged at the terrible stench. "What *is* that?" he asked. It was a foul combination of skunk, rotting fish guts, and the acrid tang of manure.

"The basilisk's hunting venom. Best get your scarf up," Aunt Phil answered.

Nate pulled his scarf over his mouth and nose. "His cave stank, but not like that." His voice came out muffled.

Aunt Phil gave him a quizzical look. "That's because it doesn't foul its own lair."

Nate tried not to stare at the destroyed village. It felt rude somehow. But it was all too real a reminder of what the basilisk could do to *them*.

An hour later, the final village came into sight. "Stop!" Aunt Phil commanded.

As Nate reined in his donkey, a confusion of noise reached his ears—shouts and cries, the sounds of running feet and stampeding animals. "The basilisk must have been sighted," Aunt Phil explained grimly. "This is it, Nate. Are you ready?" Without waiting for his reply, she dug her heels into her donkey's sides, then galloped straight for the village.

No, Nate thought. *I'm not ready.* But he followed her anyway.

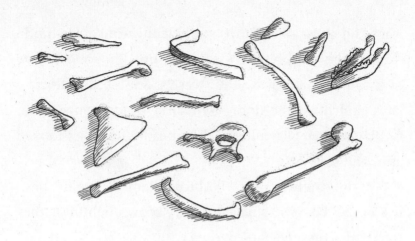

Chapter Fifteen

MUCH TO NATE'S RELIEF, Aunt Phil steered the donkeys around to the far side of the village. The area was barren; nothing but a few thorn trees and a scattering of rocks and stones. Giant boulders had tumbled down the nearby escarpment and littered the ground. "This will do, I think. See where the cliff ridge curves around? We'll take our stand there so we have something solid at our backs. But first we need to secure the donkeys someplace where they'll be safe."

They steered their mounts closer to the cliffs. Rocks were everywhere—some nearly as big as the Dhughani huts.

Aunt Phil chose one of those to hide the donkeys behind.

Once the donkeys were secure, Aunt Phil called Nate over to help her release the weasels. She undid the crate latch and lifted the door. Two furry heads popped out. Gone was their playfulness; their beady little eyes looked grim and serious.

"Go on, you two," Aunt Phil told them. "Bring the basilisk to us." Like two streaks of furry brown lightning, they raced off across the hard-packed earth.

Nate heard a sniff. He turned to his pack, where Greasle's head peeked out. "Good riddance," she muttered.

"Pull your scarf up if you're coming out," he warned.

"Not sure I wants to come out," the gremlin said .

Nate tended to agree with her, which gave him an idea. "Should I stay here with the donkeys?" he asked Aunt Phil. "To be sure they don't run off?"

Grunting, she lifted her pack. "How would you learn anything that way? Besides, you won't be in any danger. You're only to observe and learn today. Let's take up position over there, between those two rocks."

Nate turned to Greasle. "What about you? Are you staying with the donkeys or coming with us?"

"I'll come, but I'm staying in the pack." She ducked back down, and Nate heard her burrowing among his things. Wishing he could do the same, he shouldered his rucksack and followed Aunt Phil.

When he caught up to her, he asked, "What are you going to do with the basilisk once you catch it?"

"Excellent question, Nate!" Aunt Phil reached into her pack and pulled out an enormous bag. "We'll put it in this basil-sack—a bag made entirely of rue fibers. That will neutralize all its poisons long enough for us to get it back to its cave without injury."

"Okay. But how are we going to get it into the sack?" Nate didn't think the creature would hop on in just because they asked nicely.

"Ah," Aunt Phil said. "We're going to sniggle it in, that's how."

Nate stared at her. Was she speaking another one of her foreign languages?

"Here, I'll show you," she said. "We're going to spread open the basil-sack, like this."

That's when Nate saw there was a stiff wire running through the open end. It held the opening rigid, like the mouth of a cave. "Oh! I get it. He'll think it's a cave and go in."

"Not exactly, but close. We'll still have to lure it in, using a sniggle pole." She pulled an odd-looking pole from the side of her pack. With a flick of her wrist, she flung it open so that it was about six feet long. A thick line was attached, and at the end of that line, a sharp hook. "This is where you'll come in. You'll climb up onto the top of that rock there. Then I'll hand you this, but with bait on the hook to lure the basilisk our way. Your job is to dangle the bait in front of the basil-sack opening, making it look interesting and tasty. Then, once the basilisk's close enough, toss the bait inside. The beast'll go after it, and I'll pop the basil-sack closed. It'll be safely trapped inside and our job will be done."

Nate didn't think it qualified as "watching and learning," but it sounded easy enough, as long as everything went according to plan. "What will we use as bait?"

"She better not think I'll do it," Greasle muttered, creeping out of the pack.

"I've got a dead mouse here that the Dolon gave me. Are you ready to give it a try?"

Nate swallowed back the *no* that wanted to come out and said, "I guess."

"Good. Let me give you a boost so you can reach the top of that rock."

She cupped her hands and gave Nate a quick lift up. He grabbed ahold and pulled, grimacing as the rough surface scraped against his stomach.

"All settled?"

Nate looked around, surprised at how little room there was. "Yeah, I think so." He flattened himself on his belly, then took the sniggle pole from Aunt Phil.

"Now, remember, your job is to stay low and out of sight so the basilisk doesn't decide it wants you instead of the bait. I'll do the rest. Got it?"

"Got it."

"Excellent. Now, stay quiet." Aunt Phil quickly checked the basil-sack to be sure it would stay open, then hurried around to the far side and crouched between it and the rock. Nate lowered the bait in front of the sack and gave it a couple of wiggles, just to get the feel of it.

Nate saw a flash of brilliant red and green through the last huts of the village. His stomach heaved and he was afraid he was going to throw up. He glanced down at Aunt Phil, whose face was set in grim lines. "It's coming," he said.

She nodded her head to let him know she'd heard. "Remember to stay down so it doesn't get distracted by you."

Nate was only too glad to obey that particular order.

Moments later, there was an angry hiss as the basilisk emerged from the village. It was much more horrible than the picture in *The Book of Beasts*.

It was bigger than Nate thought twenty fingers would be, for one thing. Nearly as tall as Aunt Phil. And it was covered all over with scales. Its tail was thicker than Nate's leg, with a wicked point at the end. But it was the colors that burned themselves onto Nate's eyeballs—glittering green, deep red, and shining yellow. He had to squint against all that brightness. The beast's small eyes were mean looking, and when it opened its yellow beak, a forked red tongue flicked out.

The creature paused, sniffed the air, then moved forward. One of the weasels darted in front of the beast, cutting off

its path to the river. The basilisk veered in the direction of Nate and Aunt Phil.

"Start your sniggling," she whispered to him.

Nate jiggled the bait, making it bounce and dance. As planned, the movement caught the basilisk's attention. It turned its gaze in their direction. Nate ducked. He wasn't sure how far twenty paces was, but he didn't want to take any chances.

Keeping his head low, Nate peeked over the edge of the rock to see what the beast was doing. With the weasels nipping at its tail, it hissed and continued making its way toward the bait and the basil-sack.

"Steady, Nate," Aunt Phil whispered. "Keep it moving now."

Nate jiggled the bait as if his life depended on it. He could feel Greasle's head poking out of his backpack, her ragged breath warm against his neck.

The basilisk was close now, nearly to the basil-sack. Nate realized he wasn't sure when he was supposed to toss the bait into the sack. Now? He inched forward, hoping to see better so he would make sure to aim correctly. Closer, closer—he could almost see the opening. Just as he

reached the edge of the rock, it crumbled out from under him, sending a shower of loose stones down. The basilisk hissed and jerked its gaze from the bait.

"Down, Nate!" Aunt Phil yelled.

Nate flattened himself against the rock.

At the sound of her voice, the basilisk swiveled its gaze in Aunt Phil's direction. Frustrated and maddened, the beast opened its mouth and made a swallowing motion, like a cat trying to cough up a fur ball. Seconds later, a long, bright yellow stream of poison shot from its mouth straight toward Aunt Phil.

Nate saw her hit the ground. The stream of poison sailed over her head and struck the rocks behind her.

There was a loud explosion as the venom sundered the stones, sending rocks and droplets of poison raining down on Aunt Phil. Her mouth snapped shut, her eyes rolled back in her head, and she collapsed to the ground.

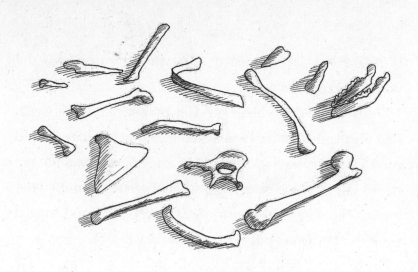

Chapter Sixteen

"*No! NO!*" Nate yelled. Panic—hot and fierce—spurted through him. Not stopping to think, he began scrambling down the rock, desperate to get to her. When he was half-way down, he realized he was a prime target for the basilisk. He scrunched his eyes shut and let go.

He landed hard, twisting his ankle and sending a bone-jarring pain up his leg. He gritted his teeth against it and crouched low, looking for the basilisk.

The two weasels were bobbing and weaving in front of the creature, drawing it away from Nate and Aunt Phil.

With the basilisk distracted, Nate threw himself on the ground next to his aunt.

"Aunt Phil?" he whispered. Her breathing was labored, her face deathly white. He glanced over his shoulder. Would the basilisk come back? He didn't know, but he had to get her to safety, just in case. Nate reached out and grabbed her heels. "I'm sorry," he murmured, then pulled and tugged until her body was safely behind the basil-sack.

Once out of sight, Nate knelt down beside her again. He reached out and gently shook her shoulder. "Aunt Phil?" he whispered.

There was still no reply. Her breath was coming in fits and starts now. He had to think of something, but what? The rue! He ran over to her huge pack and rifled through all the small leather pouches and sealed jars until he spotted the familiar leaves.

He pulled them out and raced back to his aunt's side, checking to be sure the basilisk was still occupied. The beast hissed and lunged for the weasels, who dodged and danced out of its way.

Nate crouched beside Aunt Phil, then stopped. How was

he supposed to get the rue into her mouth when she was unconscious? He couldn't just shove it in. She might choke. The only thing he could think of was to hold it under her nose. Maybe the smell alone would help.

But when he tried it nothing happened, except her breathing grew even shallower. A sharp bubble of panic rose up in his chest. She *couldn't* die. She was the only Fludd left besides him. "Wake up!" he yelled, pounding his fists on the ground. Instead of waking up, she took one last wheezing breath, then lay still.

Nate jumped blindly to his feet. He had to do something. Anything. He ran over to his backpack and dumped the contents out onto the ground. Greasle tumbled out with a howl of protest. "What is it, you great oaf!"

Nate ignored her, his eyes zeroing in on the small packet that held the phoenix egg. The words from *The Book of Beasts* leaped into his head. *A pinch of ashes from the fire of a phoenix can cure the gaze of a basilisk, the bite of a manticore, the scratch from a dragon's claw, or any human illness.*

He snatched up the egg and hurried back to Aunt Phil. He carefully unwrapped it, glad to see there was plenty of ash collected in the handkerchief. Exactly how much was a pinch? He dipped his finger into the pearly gray ash and touched it to her tongue.

For a long second, nothing happened, and then she coughed and took in a huge gulping breath. Her eyelids fluttered and color flooded back into her cheeks.

Behind him the chattering of the weasels grew frantic. A loud hiss and roar brought Nate to his feet.

The basilisk flung the weasels from its back with one hard flick of its tail, then turned its gaze to Nate. Nate ducked and the cliff beside him exploded in a small shower of scree.

"What was that?" Greasle asked, peeking out from behind Nate's rucksack.

"It's his gaze," Nate explained. "It's shattering the rocks. If we could just find a way to get rid of that, we might have a chance."

"We? What's this *we* stuff?" Greasle wanted to know. "You wake me when you get it straightened out."

"Oh no. You want to get out of here alive, don't you?"

"Course I do. But I thinks it's best if I stays in the pack until you get it taken care of." She started to scramble back

inside, but Nate grabbed her by the scruff of the neck. He froze as his gaze landed on his aviator goggles.

He blinked, then looked at the basilisk, whose poisonous gaze had just withered one of the last two remaining thorn trees. It *could* work. Maybe.

If he could get near the basilisk.

And if he could get the goggles on him.

Almost as if hearing his thoughts, the basilisk turned its bright, ugly head in Nate's direction. Nate hit the ground just in time. The problem was, Nate was too big a target. He needed to be smaller. He looked at Greasle, clutched in his hand, her eyes screwed tightly shut. Maybe . . .

Nate whistled, a short single note like Aunt Phil had

used. One of the weasels—maybe Roland—paused mid-stride and galloped over.

"Whatcha call him for?" Greasle asked.

"Because I have an idea," Nate told her. "We need to disable the basilisk's gaze. Once we do that, we'll have a chance of catching it without getting killed in the process."

"Well, good luck with that," Greasle said, diving for the rucksack.

Nate snagged her back. "Oh no. That's where you come in. I'm too big. There's no way I can sneak up on it. But you're small. And quick. Roland here can get you in close enough. If you ride on his back, he can even carry you all the way up to the basilisk's head. Then you can slip these goggles on him. I'll step in and do the rest."

"You've lost your mind, you have," Greasle said. "I ain't doing no such thing!"

Nate stared at the little gremlin. "Very well. If you're happy being stuck out here in the middle of nowhere for the rest of your life. No oil or grease or even a steam engine for hundreds of miles—"

"No, no!" Greasle said. "You can handle him."

"I can, but I need a little help." Nate held up the goggles.

Greasle looked at the weasel, who sat waiting patiently. "How do I know he won't try to eat me?"

"I'm pretty sure gremlin isn't a part of his diet."

Greasle's shoulders slumped. "Tell me what I need to do."

Nate knelt down in front of her. "The most important thing is to not touch the basilisk's skin. It's probably poisonous. Roland will get you up near its head. Once you're up there, slip the goggles over its eyes by holding the back strap, like this. That way you won't have to actually touch the beast. As soon as you snap them in place, get away quick."

Greasle took the goggles, which were nearly as long as she was, and turned to the weasel. "Did you get all that?" she asked.

Roland made a happy chittering sound and nodded his head. He squatted down so Greasle could climb on.

"Good luck," Nate told them.

"Bury me somewhere near an airstrip," Greasle said morosely. Then the weasel leaped forward and they were off.

Nate watched them go and hoped he wasn't making a mistake. He was pretty sure Aunt Phil wouldn't trust something this important to a gremlin. Unfortunately, he didn't know what she would do instead.

If only she would wake up. She was breathing steadily now, her color fully returned to normal. He allowed himself a brief happy daydream that she'd wake up in time to deal with the basilisk, but quickly gave that up when he heard an angry hiss behind him.

He turned in time to see the basilisk swing around, roaring at Roland, who was trying to crawl up the creature's lashing tail.

Sallie helped by feinting toward the basilisk's head, drawing its attention away from Roland and Greasle.

With the basilisk focused on Sallie, Roland stalked toward the tail, trying to time his movement to avoid its sharp point.

There, Nate thought. *There's* your opening.

The weasel thought so, too. He leaped onto the basilisk's back. The beast's mighty tail twitched, the flat arrow-shaped end nearly connecting with Roland. Nate heard Greasle squeal, but Roland ducked forward and made a mad dash for the basilisk's head.

"Now!" Nate yelled. Moving faster than he'd ever seen her, Greasle reached out and snapped the goggles in place. They were on!

The basilisk gave a mighty hiss and tossed its head. Greasle and Roland went flying through the air, then landed on the ground with a *thud*.

Nate's stomach dropped to the bottom of his feet. "Greasle!" he shouted.

The gremlin didn't move, but the basilisk swung its head around in Nate's direction. A big, ugly tangle of feelings rose inside Nate: sorrow, despair, guilt, anger. As he bent over to pick up the sniggle pole, he latched on to the anger. It was the least painful.

"Okay, you big overgrown snake," he said to the basilisk. "Aunt Phil didn't want you dead, but I don't care. You've done more than enough damage today."

The basilisk hissed and took a step closer. Nate jiggled the sniggle pole at it. "That's right. Pay attention to this." Nate's plan, such as it was, was to taunt the basilisk straight into the basil-sack. It wasn't much, but it was all he could think of.

The basilisk took another step forward, then another. It opened its mouth, but no hiss came out. Surely that meant it was getting ready to spit its venom! Nate dropped the pole and snatched up the mirror from the rucksack contents at his feet. He got it out in front of him just as the basilisk launched a thick stream of venom his way.

The poison struck the mirror, then arced back in the basilisk's direction. Nate peeked around the edge in time to see the poison strike a rocky overhang just behind the basilisk. Stones and rubble exploded into the air. One large stone bounced twice off the cliff, then landed on the basilisk's head with an audible *thunk*.

The basilisk swayed on its feet, then slumped to the ground.

Nate's jaw dropped open and he looked from the mirror back to the basilisk. Could it be?

Behind him, someone started to clap. He whirled around to find Aunt Phil sitting up against one of the boulders, weak but awake. She was applauding. "Oh, well done, Nate. Brilliant idea, that!"

He felt himself blush all the way to the roots of his hair. "I-I didn't know what else to do," he confessed. "Not with you unconscious."

"You did splendidly," she said.

"Thanks," he said, suddenly feeling shy. "I need to go check on Greasle."

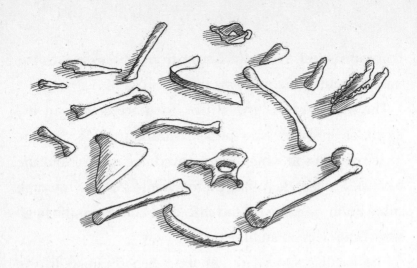

Chapter Seventeen

*T*HE GREMLIN LAY FLAT ON HER BACK, eyes closed, not moving. "Greasle?" Nate whispered.

She opened one eye. "Is it dead?"

He couldn't decide whether to shake her or hug her. "Not dead, but out cold. Because of you."

She sat up. "Because of me?"

"Yes, you were very brave." Nate gently lifted the gremlin from the ground. Sallie sat by Roland, licking him and chittering quietly. Nate reached out and gave each weasel a quick rub on the head. "You guys were great, too."

Greasle sniffed. "I think I scraped me elbow, right here, see?" She held it up for Nate to examine.

"I see," he said. "Do you want me to bandage it for you?"

Greasle perked up. "What's a bandage?"

"Here, I'll show you." Nate carried her back to his supplies still scattered on the ground and pulled out a length of gauze. He gently wrapped it around her elbow. When he was done, Greasle studied it admiringly.

"If you've seen to your gremlin," Aunt Phil said dryly, "we should probably secure the basilisk before it comes to."

"Of course!" Nate jumped to his feet, feeling guilty. He should have thought of that.

Aunt Phil pulled on her gloves and grabbed the basil-sack. Stopping long enough to grab his own gloves, Nate followed her to where the unconscious basilisk lay. Warily, Nate knelt by the beast. Asleep like this, it didn't seem nearly as terrifying. Its bright green head lolled to one side, its small forked tongue hanging out.

Aunt Phil rifled in her pack for one of the tightly sealed bottles that Nate had noticed earlier. "Chloroform," she announced, then poured some on a handkerchief and held

it against the basilisk's face. "This will ensure the beast stays unconscious until we get it back to the cave."

Together they rolled the creature into the basil-sack. It never gave so much as a twitch of its tail. Once it was safely in the bag, Aunt Phil secured the sack with a length of rope, then slung it over her donkey's back. The donkey brayed and pranced sideways, but Aunt Phil was able to calm him.

With the basilisk secured, Nate began to tremble. All the fear he hadn't had time to feel earlier now rushed through him. He didn't have time to think before, just act. But now—now he could hardly believe what he'd just done.

He'd faced the basilisk. And won. He had to sit down for a minute, just to collect himself.

Aunt Phil politely ignored him while he sat in the dirt and tried to quit shaking. After a few moments, without saying anything, she came and helped him up onto his donkey. Once he was settled, they began the trip back to the village.

Somehow, word of the basilisk's capture traveled quickly. Villagers joined their procession, dancing and cheering at being safe once again. By the time they reached the village, they were a parade. The Dolon was waiting for them.

Aunt Phil dismounted and whispered something in the Dolon's ear. He nodded twice, then clapped his hands and called out orders.

Aunt Phil motioned for Nate to follow her and the Dolon as they made their way to the basilisk's cave. "Your goggles gave me an idea," she explained. "I'm going to perform minor surgery. A little nip here and a little tuck there, and these goggles will be permanently in place. That way the basilisk's caretakers won't risk death every time they need to tend to it."

When they reached the basilisk's cave, Aunt Phil and the Dolon hauled the sack holding the king of serpents into the first cavern, where plenty of light spilled in. They laid the beast out on the top of a large, flat rock, using it as a makeshift table. The next thing Aunt Phil did was administer another dose of chloroform. She winked at Nate. "Don't want it waking up until we're good and ready."

She collected a small black bag from her pack. When she opened it, Nate saw a number of shiny steel instruments. Most of them had sharp edges. "Come and watch this, Nate," she said. Swallowing a lump that rose up in his throat, Nate inched forward.

Aunt Phil had been right about the goggles. She made two tiny snips at the side of the basilisk's head, so small Nate didn't think the beast would have noticed them even if it had been awake. Next came a few efficient stitches, and the goggles were in place.

While the basilisk was belly up on the table, Nate snuck a peek near its tail, then frowned in puzzlement. "So which is it, Aunt Phil? A boy or a girl?"

"Neither," Aunt Phil said as the Dolon laughed.

Nate glanced back at the tail again. "Neither? How can that be?"

"Basilisks are like mules, Nate. A product of two different species, a cockerel egg hatched by a serpent. They cannot reproduce and so are, for all intents and purposes, without gender."

Just then, the basilisk twitched on the table, then shuddered. "Everyone get back now," Aunt Phil ordered.

The beast yawned and tried to slither off the table. It was clumsy still and managed to roll off, looking surprised when it landed. It shook its tail and hissed. When none of them ran away, it cocked its head, as if puzzled. "Careful, there," Aunt Phil told Nate. "It will take a bit for the chloroform to wear off."

The basilisk tried hissing again. When still none of them fled, it seemed to grow bored and lurched off into the depths of its cave.

Aunt Phil turned to Nate. "Our work here is done."

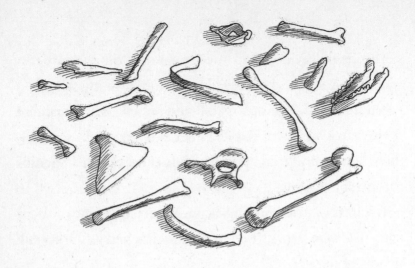

Chapter Eighteen

*T*HEY SET OUT EARLY THE NEXT DAY for the Niger River to meet Jean-Claude. Nate could hardly believe three days had passed. Hopefully, the boat would be fixed by now.

He yawned. They had stayed up late the previous night, celebrating the capture of the basilisk. He, Aunt Phil, the weasels, and even Greasle had been given a place of honor. There had been dancing and they'd roasted a goat and half a dozen chickens for the feast.

Which reminded Nate of a question he'd been meaning to ask. "Aunt Phil, isn't a cockerel a rooster?"

"Yes, Nate. It is."

"But I thought it was the hens that laid the eggs."

"Ah, excellent question. Mostly, you are right. However, very old roosters sometimes develop an egg. It is extremely uncommon, but it does happen. It is even more unusual for a serpent to find the egg and sit on it long enough to hatch it. That is why basilisks are so very rare."

"Huh," Nate said. There was so much he had to learn if he was going to be a beastologist.

They rode in silence for a while longer before Aunt Phil spoke again. "I've been thinking, Nate. Something is very wrong. We must make all haste back to England."

"What do you mean?" Nate asked.

"I believe the man at the oasis was the same one who freed the basilisk. He has known with uncanny accuracy the exact location of two very hidden beasts."

"How could that be? I thought we had the only copy of *The Book of Beasts*."

"True. There are other bestiaries, but they don't contain copies of the Fludd maps necessary to find the creatures. No, the only other source of that information is *The Geographica*."

Nate frowned, thoroughly confused. "But you said my father had the only remaining copy."

"Precisely. I have to believe that your father's and *The Geographica*'s disappearances are related to this stranger's sudden knowledge of where to find the beasts."

Nate sat up straighter on his donkey. Aunt Phil had said "disappearance," not death. As the tiniest drop of hope appeared in his chest, all his weariness left him. "So now what?" he asked.

"So now we find some answers," Aunt Phil said. "I'd like to start with that lawyer you spoke to, and your Miss Lumpton as well."

"Then what are we waiting for?" Nate said. He slapped the reins and urged his donkey forward. As if sensing Nate meant business, the donkey cooperated and broke into a trot. Aunt Phil looked startled as Nate flew past her on the path to the river.

NATHANIEL FLUDD'S GUIDE TO PEOPLE, PLACES, AND THINGS

Bamako: the capital of French Sudan.

basilisk: a creature born of a cockerel egg, incubated by a serpent or a toad. Known for its poisonous gaze and breath. Also called the king of serpents.

basil-sack: a bag or sack made entirely of rue fibers, which neutralize the basilisk's poison enough to allow the creature to be transported.

Dhughani: the descendants of the Songhay Empire who care for the basilisk.

Dolon: the spiritual leader of the Dhughani people who is responsible for taking care of the basilisk.

equator: the imaginary line that bisects the globe and divides the world into the Northern and Southern hemispheres.

Florian Fludd: Mungo Fludd's great-great-grandson. The beastologist who returned to Africa and helped a small band of refugees from the Songhay Empire relocate to the Bandigara escarpment.

Isidore Fludd: a son of Mungo Fludd. The first Fludd to visit Africa and make contact with the Songhay Empire.

magnetic north: the magnetic north pole, where compass needles point.

navigating furrows: the furrows dug in the ground in the early days of flying to help pilots navigate large land masses that had no identifying features.

Niger River: a river in western Africa, the third largest on the African continent.

Prince Henry the Navigator: a prince of Portugal who lived from 1394 to 1450 and founded a famous school of navigation. Was the force behind much of Portugal's early discoveries in Africa.

rue: an herb that is widely known to neutralize many types of poison, including the basilisk's.

Sahara: the world's largest desert, covering most of northern Africa.

Sahel: the portion of Africa that borders the Sahara Desert.

sniggle: a pole and hook used to coax beasts into or out of caves and nooks. Most widely known for its use in catching eels, beastologists have found many more uses for it.

Songhay Empire: sometimes spelled *Songhai*. One of the largest African empires, it existed from the fifteenth century to the end of the sixteenth century.

Sudan: a geographic area just south of the Sahel that spans the African continent.

Sunni Ali: the ruler of the Songhay Empire from 1464 to 1492.

telegram: a method of communication using Morse code to send a message through the wires that is then translated into words.

Timbuktu: important city famed for its gold and riches during the medieval Mali and Songhay empires.

true north: the geographic North Pole.

Wadi Rumba: a small outpost in Arabia.

weasel: a small, long mammal in the same family as mongooses. Playful and a good hunter. The natural enemy of the basilisk.

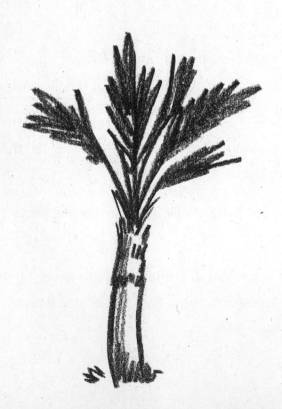